Lucky Goes to Dog School

Story by Beverley Randell
Illustrations by Joseph Qiu

Dad and Ruby
and Lucky the dog
went to the store.

"A car is coming," said Ruby.

"Woof!" said Lucky.

"Come here, Lucky," shouted Dad.

"Come here, Lucky," shouted Ruby.

"Naughty dog!" said Dad.
"Come here!"

DOG TRAINING
SCHOOL
SATURDAYS
10AM

"Look at this, Ruby," said Dad.

"Look! A dog school!"

Dad and Ruby and Lucky
went in.

"Woof! Woof!" said Lucky.

"Sit," said the teacher.

"Sit, Lucky," said Dad. "No, Lucky. **Sit!**"

The teacher came to help.

"Sit like this,"

he said to Lucky.

"Sit. **Sit!**"

"Woof!" said Lucky.

"Sit, Lucky," said Dad.

"Sit.

   Sit, you naughty dog!

   Stay with me and sit **down**!"

Dad and Ruby and Lucky
went home.

"Sit, Lucky," said Ruby.
"Sit. **Sit!**
Good dog!
Dad! Look at Lucky!"

"Good dog!" said Dad.

"Woof, woof!" said Lucky.